Thrift

Thrift

Barbara Louise Ungar

WordTech Editions

Published by WordTech Editions
P.O. Box 541106
Cincinnati, OH 45254-1106

Typeset in Dutch by WordTech Communications LLC,
Cincinnati, OH

ISBN: 1932339647
LCCN: 2004106435

Poetry Editor: Kevin Walzer
Business Editor: Lori Jareo

Visit us on the web at www.wordtechweb.com

for Noah

and
in memory of

Jon Greenberg

Acknowledgments

Grateful acknowledgment is made to the editors of the following publications, in which some of these poems first appeared, some in slightly different form:

Salmagundi: "Still Life with Times" and "With You in the Thrift Shop of My Dreams"

The Minnesota Review: "The Only Woman I Know"

The Cream City Review: "Nonalogy"

The Sow's Ear Poetry Review: "Jesus in the Art Hospital"

Global City Review: "Magic Carpet Edition"

The Literary Review: "Ode to the Grace Building"

Whalelane: "From the Cutting Room Floor"

Heartfelt thanks to all who helped: Frank Bidart, Ann Lauterbach, Peg Boyers, Eva Hooker, Ann Settel, Stuart Bartow, Naton Leslie; Paul Elisha, Barbara Kaiser, Joseph Kraussman, Sue Oringel, Sara Wiest, Gretchen Ingersoll, Hollis Seamon, and Tobias Seamon. Many thanks to the College of Saint Rose for sabbatical and release time to complete this book.

Contents

III. Thrift

Thrift, *sb.* 1 [f. THRIVE + T *suffix* 3a: cf. *drift, gift, rift, weft,* etc; also ON. *thrift,* occasional synonym of *thrif,* thriving condition, well-doing, prosperity. . .]

1. The fact or condition of thriving or prospering; prosperity, success, good luck; in early use sometimes = fortune (good or bad); luck. . .

b. Means of thriving; industry, labour, profitable occupation. Now *dial.*

c. Prosperous growth, physical thriving.

d. Growing pains, *dial.*

I. Knowledge

Magic Carpet Edition

from *The Book of Knowledge,* Grolier, 1953

Wonder Questions:

1) Does light die away? 2) Does the moon
pull the sea? 3) What makes us sneeze?
4) Who invented the zipper? 5) Where do all the stones
come from? 6) Why does furniture make noise
at night? 7) What *is* linoleum?
8) What was wrong with Achilles'
heel? 9) Is it darkest
just before dawn? 10) Is it true that sound
goes on forever? 11) Will the world
become like the moon? 12) Why do our voices sound
hollow in an empty hall?

Answers:
12) To answer this
question, we might begin by asking ourselves why we use
the word "hollow" to describe our voices. 8) Nothing. 3)
It's a reflex. 11) Our earth will probably, in time,
become a dead world in the heavens,
with not a breath of air. 1) Light always dies
away when its source ceases, yet light
might travel on forever, spreading like ripples in a pond. 2) Yes.
6) It's always groaning; we only listen at night
when we can't sleep. 9) No. 5) Stones are
pieces of broken rock. 7) Linseed oil & cork.
4) Whitcomb L. Judson. 10) No sound

lasts forever *as a sound*. Yet nothing
is ever lost: the energy of its waves must go on in some way forever

As in Dreams You Swim with Whales

You didn't even know it was endangered, it was so

friendly every snorkelling tourist at the Mauiian
visited the great sea tortoise
in the reef off the hotel beach.

You had to search and search the strange underwater

garden without landmarks
until (your gasp
magnified by snorkel gear)

it slipped out from greygreen coral—

gliding upwards with majestic
slowness and calm,
flapping its legs like wings,

the great turtle rose to the surface

where you dead-man-floated
till you could meet those ancient
netted eyes that seemed scrutable.

You reached out and stroked the satin shell

before, with a flick of its wing-
like legs, it vanished. Next time, it seemed to beckon
you to play, *C'mon,* swimming slow

enough for you to follow, enchanted,

to its secret lair
where you could frolic with seals and dolphins
as in dreams you swim with whales

until you picked your head up from the water's pillow

and saw how the tortoise was leading you on and out
into open ocean, far from the curving hotel strip,
the tiny umbrellas. The tide already strong against you

ripping you out. Was this not your friend

but the snake of the sea
wreaking its small revenge on your stupid race?
Seeing how far you would go before you realized you had gone too far.

You didn't know you weren't supposed to touch it.

Nonalogy

I want my grandmother, Anya, but she's in bed
with a wolf. The wolf eats Anya up. The wolf
is Anya: she ate my father's

left eye, and stuffed cabbage with his heart,
the poor woodcutter. She came
sledding down from Transylvania in her coffin,

swam the Atlantic and stalked across America,
a werewolf frisking at her shadow. She
can teach me. She knows everything, being dead

and undead: Anya fattens on my thin blood
and kicks sharpest at the full moon, when I
skip off to find her,

when my hair's thicker, and I'm
starving. I need to know how to live
with this wolf. See—there he is—loping easily

alongside no matter how fast I run, in and out
the tangled wood, tongue lolling, garlic breath
grinning at my little hood

red as blood when it first meets air.
Smarter than the three pigs, Grandma, you
invited him right into your

nightgown. You old hairy thing, madwoman,
what big eyes
you have. I know you'll eat me. Just let me

tell you a story first: how
when we're in the beast's belly,
underneath your flannel,

the woodcutter's ax rings, a bloody
door swings open, and you and I,
hand in hand, spring out unscathed.

Formic

After arranging the peonies, I scoop
crazed ants off the counter

with delicate paper coaxings, and,
by my third transport

across the grass to the peony bush, wonder
if they could find their own way

home from the front
steps (like pets who navigate

the continent) or if they'd be devoured
by enemy armies (an ant *Iliad*)

and what tales
do they tell the colony

of alien abduction
(the A-Files?)

and of the strangeness of formica
and this paper plane.

Still Life with Times

I had breakfast with my past
present & future today at Claude's. The past
went white, mouth tight & twisted.

Can I join you?
Of course. The past turned
charming, we sipped cappucino, the present

skimmed the newspaper of the past.
I gave him the postcard from Lago di Como, *When*
will we lunch at Tremezzo again? Ah,

never. *The lake wasn't that blue,*
said the past without his glasses.
The past traded quips with the present

& the future & I laughed—my past likes my
present, my future likes my past—perhaps
there's hope. We finished our croissants. The past

escaped, like always, the tears
streamed down his face at Ellis Island. Like mine
in Prague. *It's hard to accept the pastness*

of the past. He says, *You sound like a cross*
between Heidegger and Adam. The present
calls later from a pay phone on Mott Street—

Chinese and honking. I'm in tears. *Wait
for me,* the future says. I'm like,
I hate this. He's like, *Put some pictures of herons*

& cranes on your fridge. He says, *I
love you,* and the line goes dead,
my *I-love-you* lost in the wire.

If I stand on one leg quietly and still
will the present turn into a future I can live with
or will the present & future turn

into my past? And how to
stop them? Stop it.
Grey water. Watch for fish.

Picasso to Malraux, 1937

masks   magic things   mediators
against everything   against
unknown threatening spirits   Negro fetishes

I understood   I too am against
everything   everything is unknown

everything is an enemy!   Everything!

Why I was a painter   weapons
to help them   tools   we give
spirits form   we become

independent   spirits   emotions
the unconscious   they're all the same

alone in that awful museum

masks   dolls   dusty mannekins
made by redskins   *Les Desmoiselles
d'Avignon*   my first exorcism

Da Capo

Decades pass,
I play piano again.

Upon waking, when
I close my eyes,

sepia sheets of music
flicker, black notes

dancing (like calendar
pages in old movies to show

time, but faster, rapid-
eye-movement or strobe)

wherever that dark
screen *is*: "behind my lids"

or "in my head," as if
homunculi or elves—the "Brownies"

framed over Mrs. Cummins's
baby grand countless years ago—

had been pulling and rifling
faded files all night to find

everything needful, like Bach
Inventions, still there.

PhD Apron

When you brought your dissertation (on Dickinson)
bound in blue & gold, she met you at their hotel-
room door with a graduation gift: an apron.

Beige, with a bib, perky red & blue flowers,
ears of grain. It said, *You can't escape. You may think*
you have, but you will never make it out of My

Kitchen. You will wear Me like chains. Everyone needs
to eat, even you, Ms. College Professor. You
think you can think your way out of this. No one can

think her way out of this. It comes far before thought.
It is food, thirst, milk, misery. I gave you life.
I gave you suffering. I give you myself. Now

Cook in Me.

Garment

I once sewed that lemon-yellow
polyester bellbottom pantsuit,
and the harlequin culotte jumper, half-

navy, half-lime, with contrasting
pockets, straps, and topstitching.
No wonder my first marriage

had to end. I'd be in it still,
the favorite dress you wear every day
till it falls apart—the one from Rhodes

I loved, white with black swallows . . .
But married, you make and wear
one suit between you, so if one

runs off in the trousers, the other
gets stuck with the jacket, or goes naked.
Is it harder for men? We all hanker

after something new, a change of fabric
or cut. Not like he thought
he could find a better fit, but

in disarray after Mamie died, he tore
the suit in two, as the Orthodox
rend the garment in mourning.

I mended the pieces
till, no matter how carefully
you patch, the fabric

disintegrates beneath the needle.
I don't sew anymore,
don't trust my hand or eye.

A *shmata.* Rag of shame.

The Nun-Cruise

The way Sister Faith stares at my hem-
line & neckline makes me feel
like the whore of Babylon, or a ripe

fig about to burst its seams
pierced by her gaze. Is she queer, I ask Christina,
who spent much of her childhood face-

down on the floor in the shape of a cross
praying for stigmata. Christina calls it the nun-
cruise, the gauntlet she had to run

every morning walking into school.
Still, I understand the desire. For years
I prayed devoutly to the burglar alarm

in Temple Israel, mistaking that high-pitched
ringing no one else seemed to hear
for the voice of God. By 14, I was an existentialist.

After Jon told me, over scrambled
eggs in the East Village, *I'm dying,*
I fasted for a week, until late one night

my body radiated light like a golden
Buddha, a pearl strung on breath, the same
breath that strings the stars.

Superluminal

As if someone looking through a window
at home were to see a man slip and fall
on a patch of ice while crossing the street
well before witnesses on the sidewalk
saw the mishap occur—nothing can travel
faster than that, according to conversation
at sophisticated wine bars, in hopes
of finding a chink in Einstein's armor.
It looks like a beautiful experiment,

said Dr. Ciao about Dr. Wang's
mind-bending work: a pulse of light
pushed through a transparent chamber so fast
it exits the chamber even before it enters.
Light can travel in opposite directions,
like a pocket of congestion on a highway
which can propagate back from a toll
booth as rush hour begins, even as
all the cars are still moving forward.

The outgoing wave just leaves early
—already traveled sixty feet
from the chamber—before the peak
of the incoming wave
arrives. This is a special property
of light itself, which is different
from a brick. A brick
could not travel so fast
without creating truly big problems.

No fundamental principles have been smashed.

A pulse of light somehow jumped forward in time.

This problem is still open
said the ingenious Italian group.
But not even Dr. Nimtz believes
that the trick will allow one to reach back in time.
Sadly, but not beyond it, he said.

To My First Address

To: 5232 Stevens Avenue South,
Minneapolis, Minnesota—
your numbers engraved first
and last, indelible as the fat black Magic
Marker, with its intoxicating, forbidden smell, I snuck
from the junk drawer (in the front hall on cool green
tiles, heart racing) to inscribe them in *Spot the Dalmation Pup:*
some of the S's and 2's got confused and had to be done
twice to get them facing in the right direction.
Four great joys: to know where you are,
to know how to write, to own
this book, and to disobey.

II. Illusion

The Magician's Assistant

There he goes again, sawing her in two.
After the spangly parade of breasts,
showgirl legs and smiles, she climbs into the box

willing as a bride of Dracula.
She trusts him. He won't hurt her.
We believe it, too, although we like

to watch. But this time the box
is buried in leaf-strewn dirt
where no one can see him

slip in his saw and go at it, or
haul her up by an arm—just the top
half, still talking. The trick

will be to put her back together.
As if it were a cartoon, or a dream
she could wake from, into some other life.

The Grace Building

Clouds cruise by, slow sharks
scraping their undersides
on the Chrysler steeple,
gunmetal blue, huge over us
scuttling the floors of these stale aquariums.

How do you do it?
Nijinsky said, *I jump up,*
I stay there a little while,
then I come down.

The sharks swim off, leaving blue sand
scalloped by waves overturned above us.
The air in whitecaps, blown hard against black glass—
why does the rain sideways blow?
High in this tower, a broken angel weeps.
The poet with mangled hands asks,
What's between inside & outside?

Glass, poems, the infinitely beveled edge
where something comes out of nothing, snow,
where Nijinsky crashes, a bird, betrayed.
Great veils gust across the lonely office towers,
blue spires, bridges & Uncle Walt's ferry,
the smudged shores. Yellow light in each cubicle,
an Advent calendar where no window opens.

This is the belly of a whale, sloped white
stone & black glass fluking on 42nd Street.

Rising from Times Square, the distorted
rant of some lost tribe in black
leather and studs, the call to prayer
in this city of wandering Jews, the only place
I feel at home, among the homeless . . .

That gold tower torched by late sun
fades into the blue pool of neon, where night
swims away, holding the seed of sleep and insect wings,
stars, singing, wine, panthers, snowmobiles,
urine, fingerprints of the dead, Ann-Margret movies,
swans, Italian shoes, fresh-cut
foreskins, oceans of tea, your single
white hair, the scar on her knee, butterflies,
purses, mushrooms, lamps, each wrinkle,
all the shades of twilight, Pampers, escarole,
pipesmoke, jellyfish, Aunt Vera's vases,
footprints on the moon, geometry,
breath smoking in autumn, every lost
sock and pen, endless weeping . . .

Here on the fortieth floor
of Grace, if we dared speak, might we not
fly like bodies sucked out plane windows by the vacuum or bomb,
like snowflakes, or Nijinksy
soaring out through the paper window of the stage set?

Self-Diagnosis

I have had very peculiar and strange
experiences. I do not always

tell the truth. I have never been sorry
that I am a girl. I have not lived

the right kind of life. I like poetry.
I do not like everyone I know. I am

fascinated by fire. I have used alcohol
excessively. I often feel as if things

were not real. I feel unable to tell
anyone all about myself. I have strange

and peculiar thoughts. I used to like
hopscotch. I drink an unusually large

amount of water every day. My face
has never been paralyzed. People say

insulting and vulgar things about me.
I have had some very unusual religious

experiences. Sometimes at elections
I vote for men about whom I know

very little. Someone has been trying
to influence my mind. There never was a time

in my life when I liked to play
with dolls. I would like to hunt

lions in Africa. I like to keep people
guessing what I'm going to do next.

I am made nervous by certain animals.
Even when I am with people I

feel lonely much of the time. These days
I find it hard not to give up hope

of amounting to something. I do not have
a great fear of snakes. I could be happy

living all alone in a cabin
in the mountains or woods. I believe

I am a condemned person.
I have never had a vision.

I have no fear of water.
I am a special agent of God.

Eve & Snake

I never want to leave here, so
when we must go, I'll make my
skin a gift for you, a soft

white glove left
hanging from the bedpost.
Like an adder, I'll rub against

twig, root, rock—any hard thing
in my path—unrolling like a stocking
till it catch on a branch, say, as I dart away

leaving it behind, glinting,
diaphanous, spent,
like a condom leaking seed.

You have taught me all I need
to grow a new skin, bigger, more
beautiful than the one before.

The Only Woman I Know

I'm fat. I think I'm fat. I always
think I'm fat. I know I'm not
fat but I think I am. I was fat
once, sort of. It was the Pill.
I hated myself, cried all the time.
Still, I'm the only woman I know
who hasn't had an abortion.
When I look in the mirror
naked, I tuck in the backs of my
upper thighs with my hands and say,
There. But—they never stay.
No one sees what I see in the mirror:
mainly the unsightly bulge at the top
of my thighs. I think, *Lip-o-suction*.

My sisters are skinny, but always
say they're fat. They're almost
anorexic. When I say I feel
fat and they're so skinny, they
say I'm skinnier. I say they're crazy,
they're the skinny ones and I'm
fat. They say I'm crazier, I'm the
skinny-malinx and they're disgusting
fat blobs, when I can see how
skinny and gorgeous they are,
but not me. Finally I say, can
I possibly be as skinny

and crazed as they are? They say
Yes. I'm amazed. Okay, so
I'm crazy—but I still think I'm fat.

Venom

> The word "venom" . . . began as the simple word *wen,*
> meaning to wish or will, leading more or less directly to
> "win." Along the way, a fork led to "venus," "venery," and
> "venerate," all indicating varieties of love. The love potion
> was called *venin,* and somehow gradually acquired today's
> sense of venom.
>
> —Lewis Thomas, *The Medusa and the Snail*

I don't want to write this, I don't want to give you
one more second of my life. My once-most-beloved-turned-to-pus,

I must expel you to heal.
How many years of irritation make pearl?

I hate to dream of you. You come crying,
a child or very small,
twisted or with open sores; I'm still living with you, hope
I don't have to kiss or fuck you—I wake furious.

I want you out of me. For
good. What to do with these images?
If I could tear them from my head like hair, I would.

I have no sense of smell, and a rotten
memory. I wish I could forget
your name. I'm waiting for the past
to catch up, or to wither and drop off like a lizard's tail.

I don't want to open the box. The trip pictures.

We carried a snake-bite kit
around the world for years, never
used it. We were happy: we smiled a lot.

Your life, a zillion tales
coiled inside me, useless—I eject
the stillborn.

I *will* forgive you. I want all those years
not to have been
wasted. I'm waiting to hear
you've had a baby with your new wife, or dropped dead.

For Jon, on My 45th Birthday

In my dream, you and I
dance together again, all
year. You are beautiful
as in your short life.

In the second dream, B. and I cut
our beloved cat in two, pick up
the halves, still alive,
and mourn our terrible mistake.

In the third, B. drives off
with my purse and everything
else, like the last one, leaving me
screaming on the street.

You and I understand
in dreams, old friends return: your golden
face streaked with tears
over a spat with some lover.

We're happy to see each other again.
You never died.

The Green Girls

You haunt our house, three sisters,
as in any tale. You make the plants grow
three times around the windows. Spinsters,

you held the fort. You chased away
all my rivals. Like the spider-
webs in the rosebushes, frail, you let

nothing by you, and can only be
seen from certain angles: a glint of light,
a whitish tissue, mostly air—a turn

of the head, and you vanish. Twelve years
you've watched him sleep, stirring
dust in the corners, lightly

tracing his lavish mouth, his arms
flung overhead, his specifically male grace.
A man like that improves a bed,

a house, a garden: how well he tends your roses.
You watched over him all those nights
he drank alone. Sisters, you delivered him

to me, whole. And I thank you.
Though you do like to play pranks: breaking
things, using his voice to wake me

when he's gone, making my green
pen run out of green ink
when I try to write your names.

Jesus in the Art Hospital

Església de Santa Maria del Mar, Barcelona

1. *lunes*

The church is mostly dark.
Such light as pierces
high slits of stained glass (pigeons'

shadows flitting past)
against the gloom.
In a niche

a twisted Jesus,
every Jew broken
on the rack, or heretic

drawn in four, down the years like bone
piled upon bone, arching back
into a gothic past of priests,

punctual as Spring, preaching
"Christ-killers"—
pogroms ignite: synagogues

stuffed with the singing dead,
smoke-spewing crematoria and
KKK crosses livid on front lawns—

strange fruit
hung from living trees.

2. *martes*

  "Sant Christ"

  "Miraculosament salvat
  de l'incendi de 1936"

An empty cross
covered in plastic, like good furniture
unused, laid down on sawhorses

in its niche, while next door
under the piteous gaze of his perfect, painted mother
he lies on a table

covered with white paper and stains,
surrounded by surgical instruments, lights
and extension cords.

Six young women in lab coats
have rolled him over
in his beige loincloth, arms outstretched

beyond the table, overhead and behind like wings.
They stroke his grain with bare fingertips
and tiny brushes; one drums on his arm, laughing.

They're at work, concentrating hard, but far
from reverent. They might be doing nails.
Mary looks down from the wall, her lovely hands

raised in the mildest of *oi veys*, toward these girls,
who look at least as young as she does, handling
her son—surely the hardest worked

body that ever was. They giggle and stroll
out in jeans and sneakers beneath their stained
white coats to smoke on the steps in the sun.

3. *miércoles*

       The holes in his hands
are empty.

      His blood is wood.
                  He cannot
lower his arms.

       Shocking
to see him like this, lying down
on the job.

They tend him with such exquisite care,
as I used to mend my stuffed animals
when worn by too much love.

How helpless he looks, stuck
on his back, waiting for mere
humans to nail him up

again. Imagine that job:
having to refit the nails
and hoist him high on his mast

like a bleeding sail.

This Fall

the geese keep flying North.
Global warming or some ominous
circling in their flight
plans beyond our ken?

Hearing their melancholy chorus
I rush out in slippers to stand in the yard
and crane till their calligraphy
disappears upriver into cloud.

Their cries sound distressed
as if they knew
they were going the wrong way.

Do they have stupid leaders too
whom they follow, honking
(they know better) to their doom?

Mrs. Johnson

In Minneapolis in May, Mrs. Johnson
stepped out the door, scissors in hand,
straw hat tied over her white hair,
ancient as Atropos among lilies
of the valley massed like Lilliputian
armies bearing green shields and spears

hung with white carillons against the side
of the house, creamy stucco like cottage cheese
with chives and tomatoes from the garden.
In deep backyard shade, under the maple,
she stooped in her starched housedress to sever
spears of bells, leaves wide as green blades,

laid each bundle down
in her basket, while the poplars
danced, their leaves flipping like coins
in the breeze, light green, then silver, endlessly
rippling like Minnehaha Creek
running low over golden stones.

Nothing happened in Minneapolis—
elms arched out from both curbs, holding
hands over the middle of the street, calm
lines of dancers under whose joined
arms one sashays solo: Mrs. Johnson,
with her basket of lilies of the valley,

dressed up to catch the Nicollet bus
downtown to the bridal shops. Not
much else—you rode the neighbor's iron
horsehead hitching post beneath the pines,
following your infant desire like the twinings
of Tangletown on your bike, a glittery

green, hand-me-down Raleigh, to Lake
Harriet to swim with the six-foot sturgeon
past the rose gardens and bandstand
where sailboats swung above their moored
reflections, or flop on the grass to write a poem
called *Rain* . . . The anomie of staring

out the window at the backyard next door
where Mrs. Johnson lived and died so quietly, so
ladylike, with no first name, never
suspecting you would later resurrect her
as a Fate. She was replaced by the Premacks,
the handsome, harddrinking Star-Trib reporter

who died young, while you waited
for something to happen, besides baby-
sitting, scaring yourself with *In Cold Blood*,
and fifty-cent movies at the Parkway—
waiting for you knew not what, to leave, go
somewhere, any coast, California,

around the world. Now you've been
everywhere, and lost everything, it's all
the same—all the elms came down,
felled by shrouds of worms, like the rain
forest, the Indians at Wounded Knee,

Mr. Premack in his prime, our circle

games on twilight lawns: *All fall down!*
As if nothing happened. You can still
grab your bike, go sailing down the hill
at top speed, and there it is—and
there—springing up like an army from dragon's
teeth, lilies of the valley growing wild in deep shade,

covering the backyard and all its graves
of dimestore turtles, hamsters and birds,
everything mourned and forgotten,
ringing their white bells silently, fragrantly,
till Mrs. Johnson steps out of her back
door with a long black scissors in her hand.

III. Thrift

2. Savings, earnings, gains, profit; acquired wealth, estate, or substance. *arch.*

3. Economical management, economy; sparing use or careful expenditure of means; frugality, saving.

4. A name given to various plants.

    ... e.g. Great Thrift, Plantain Thrift, Lavender Thrift, Prickly Thrift.

5. *attrib.* and *Comb.,* as (in sense 3) *thrift club, society,* etc.; (in sense 4) *thrift edging*; thrift-box, -pot, a box or pot in which savings are put.

It Is Better to Say I'm Suffering than to Say This Landscape Is Ugly

—Simone Weil

a child

driven through that merciless country
vomiting at regular intervals

saw

a starved yellow dog lap the pink pool of american lunch
from gas station dust like the unknown delicacy it truly was

yelping in a jalopy men run down another dog the color of dust

a bloody naked jew haul wood through gilt-encrusted basilicas
baby slung from hunched back   a crone hawking fools' gold on the steps

flocks of boys squabbling for pennies or candy *watchercar meester*

squatting in the desert women make tortillas out of *nada nada*
grinning children hold up armadillos by the road

no context   but the fleeing shadow of a blue Oldsmobile

For the Town Clerk

The second marriage is the triumph of hope over experience.
                                            —Dr. Johnson

The last envelope
in the last corner of
the last drawer of the desk,
shuffled under students' love letters (one earnest
proposal, from Hing, with return postage) dear Jon
letters, homemade valentines, defunct
address books, pictures of estranged friends'
kids, indecipherable postcards,
letters from Charles, long dead of AIDS,
wedding photos, trip photos &, in a pink
gift bag stamped PANDORA'S
BOX, a garter &
sugar packet from the Paris honeymoon—
kaleidocopic bits you
meant to do something with
still undone, undiscarded, sifting
down to his hand-
writing, the last nasty
exchanges over money & promises unkept—
LOOK says the envelope: at last

the divorce papers
you shoved there, without hope.

Guidebook

You thought it was dead,
a huge, sleek sausage
on a long, hot griddle of sand

& cautiously crept up till it stirred,

grumbled in its sleep
& wallowed a bit closer to the surf,
miles from mall & condo,

down an old pineapple plantation's

dirt roads, where locals fished—
twisted pines, volcanic
cliffs, the Pacific

crashing up through spoutholes in the rock.

Visiting Kauai without a helicopter trip,
the guidebook said, *is like visiting*
the Sistine Chapel & not looking up.

So you shelled out, but more thrilling

was meeting that lone, wild
seal on its deserted beach. The pilot
said it must have been a monk seal, common once:

tourists often think they're sick

& try to shove them back into the ocean
or splash them, nocturnal solitaries
sleeping in the sun.

He had nothing to do with the military

now & had stopped watching TV years ago,
he said. *People come, I take them up, people go.*
As long as I don't read the news—

This is Paradise—

Eros Theory

He was Dutch, almost ugly, a chaos
physicist who liked my dress
on the subway, its fifties pick-up-

stix print, & after too much
red wine, he was almost handsome
when he showed me his meticulous

photorealistic drawings
of vulva, & when he
exclaimed, *Just like I knew*

it would look, & of a certain beauty
mark, *I bet no man who sees that*
ever forgets it.

Over-reverent, or guilty
over a girlfriend in Amsterdam, he
couldn't, & I left with a book on chaos

theory. Actual lovers I was crazed
about I never think of, & my ex
I'm happiest to forget,

but most days I think
of him, the nameless
chaos physicist, & smile

in the shower at that birth
mark no one else ever
mentioned, if they noticed—

hurricane
touched off

by such light wings.

Another Minneapolis Poem

What better place in America to die?
Berryman did, in his wild beard,
leapt off a bridge into the mid-

winter Mississippi. I might have passed him,
crossing the old U of M bridge
between dance class and orthodontia:

he would have seen nothing,
just some skinny, dark-eyed girl,
unfuckable, her rabbity

overbite, and I would not have known
who he was. But if I had,
I could have offered him a carrot

from my lunch, stroked his mad
patriarchal beard, tried to soothe the trembling
skin from jumping out of its suit, or

invited him home to Dad's
diffident and meager sherry, Mom's
bridge mix and overanxious laugh . . . Or

would I have been afraid of him
weeping in his great coat, declaiming to invisible
companions, unable to bear another

day without drink or the hell
the drink would haul in its wake? No,
I would have loved him. My father

taught me to love men who suffer
unbearably and hide it
badly, men who work all day, alone,

and return to snowy lawns, with no hat
in the bitterest cold, in beige overcoats
and dark galoshes. *There is no loneliness*

like theirs. I want to pet them like ponies'
velvet noses, murmur as I feed them
sugar or proffer a nipple—
                  C'mon, John,

read your Hopkins—stop taking
yourself so goddamned serious-like.
Stay with me, pal, don't go—

                  But how can one know,
as Horace cautioned (re: Empedocles'
leap into Aetna), whether saving a poet

guarantees a good
life? Or that the poet won't just
try again? And again

he stumbles over
the rusted guard rail, sobs, and
rises, transparent, through the sepia

frozen landscape, still arguing
with God and Mr. Bones, as the fluttering
overcoat hits the ice

empty, sucked down
by the irresistable
pull of the Mississippi River,

far colder than any man can feel.

Barbarian

To write poetry after Auschwitz is barbaric.
                    —Adorno

What should we do?
                    Fall
silent?
        Like those you were forced

to dig up—living
                    mouths
sealed
        with plaster,

they could breathe through
                            their
noses
        but not scream, while being

tortured, or speak.
                        Even
Nazis
        feared words.

So you're compelled
                    to
tell
    and we to repeat:

let this poem be
              the
echo
    of a silent scream

Kaddish for Jon

Jon, you're turning into a fucking saint
I said, when you returned to the East
Village from the Other Side, streaming
golden light. You laughed & said
I know. You'd chosen to come back
to your work, holistic
treatment of AIDS, knowing nothing
but what could be gleaned in the laboratory
of your body, refusing
drugs that kept your brother alive
to dance.

> *He who dwells within all living bodies*
> *remains forever indestructible.*
> *Therefore the truly wise mourn neither*
> *for the living nor for the dead.*

Deaf & emaciated, you came to Woodstock:
we ate six meals a day & nonstop guacamole,
did yoga, read *Gita* & *Tao.* One morning
you stepped into the cabin, face wet
with tears:
> *I can hear*
> *the wind in the trees.*

I watched you
letting go of your
self, your lithe shape
that loved to dance & sing.

Yitgadal v'yitkadash sh'may rabah—
Magnified & sanctified may His great name be
in the world that He created, as He wills . . .

At Saint Vincent's, still shining
in your coma
you lay surrounded by stricken
disciples. I fanned you with a black lace fan
Laura had brought from Barcelona
& recited our favorite verse from the *Tao*,
the one that drove everyone else nuts
for months on your answering machine:

> *When you realize where you come from,*
> *you naturally become tolerant,*
> *disinterested, amused,*
> *kindhearted as a grandmother,*
> *dignified as a king.*
> *Immersed in the wonder of the Tao,*
> *you can deal with whatever life brings you,*
> *and when death comes, you are ready.*

Your baby brother Neil is bigger
& older now than you
will ever be, more famous, less
handsome, still
here. When he dances
you in your coma,
he stands in darkness, dead-still, eyes
shut under a single spot, eyebrows &
hands (curled like a baby's) barely
twitching

Entrances/Chambers II

   after a sculpture by Tom Schottman

slit
         whence we came

clay
         where we return

chambers
            to pass the hours between

four-tiered, four-sided tower
number of wholeness
and of death

rear view: round eyeholes
vertical nose-slit
as if inside a mask,
skull chamber
or chador—

peering out
through battlements
walled city
women's quarters

a head
         crowning

         comes full circle to

a box

that keyhole
you alone can
and will
unlock

The Green Girls at Work

The garden, a dry
tangle of weeds & flowers
soon to be mown
down. The nights are cold, the days

summery. Here
& there, a flower
: two Icelandic poppies,
the orange-gold of happiness,

hardy violas &
on the Constance Spry long
gone to hips, a perfect
pale pink rose

& another bud—no,
two—pointed green brushes
dipped in deeper pinks—
the Green sisters at work.

One rose apiece they sent,
treble message not to fret
about death, the inevitable
seasons & loss,

for where they dwell
in the dirt even spinsters become
the force that through the green fuse
drives these buds & blooms

from that scraggy bush
they planted
about a hunded years ago
when they lived here.

From the Cutting Room Floor

babs—

i know you've been waiting to hear
it's true
there is no time   no here
the movie unspools
all frames play eternally

here we are at 14, meeting in the back of a crowded vw bug
singing joni mitchell and talking about god
here i am, telling you *i love you*, and you say *jon,*
you're gay—don't you know? you're really in love
with dan   i say *i'm in love with you both*

cut to you and me and dan skinny-dipping
in lake harriet, fumbling for our clothes in the car—police
flashlight—i'm trying to untangle my overalls and hide
the pot—you unroll the back window
may i help you, officer?

here we are getting stoned for the first time
time bends
you hear your parents on the phone as squirrels
chattering with needless grey anxiety
how i hear you
you should worry less
write more

here we are in rome, on the banks of the tiber:
i'm breaking larry's heart, aldo's breaking mine   cut to
woodstock: *your* aldo is breaking *your* heart, so i make you
piss on his lawn at night   here we are
diving into the quarry—wide awake
in ice-green water—that perfect summer day
you wish would never end
it doesn't

here we are, eating guacamole in eternity

here i am, testing positive

here is my postcard, sadfaced, ringletted
renaissance angels playing lutes
don't get around much any more

flashback to me at 17 telling you the play i will write
and perform on broadway ends with my
suicide on stage
here is the final tearjerking scene

and encore
my funeral circus: men i love carry my body in an open coffin
in a purple satin halter top down 1st avenue
love the crowd in the park   thanks for the poem

here we are at 35, on your stoop on east 5th street
you're leaving glenn after 15 years, i'm dying, we're laughing
about how you told me i was gay, we're

singing joni mitchell and talking about god
as always—

   ciao, bella

     love,
      jon

The Thrift Shop of My Dreams

Tout passe, tout casse, tout lasse.

Everything's used, everything's worn, everything's
been here before, belonged to someone
else, held another body in its arms. Everything

changes hands. Threads outlast us: the container
& the thing contained. Like a dance, trading
partners down the line: do si do and an

allemande left. Who are you
this time? One man melds into
another, into a woman, she's

my sister, who's my mother, she's   I prefer
the used, the worn, the broken in: like
eating dirt, or library books, well thumbed,

corners rounded & softened with use.
Other women's hands washed these, stroked your
hair, your shirts, your cock. Now mine. I want to be

your one & only forever, no one
here before, though I know they were,
& are, with you in the thrift shop

of your dreams. *There is no possession,*
only desire. And this, too, has been
said before. There is no end

Notes

I. Knowledge
"Magic Carpet Edition" is a found poem, from *The Book of Knowledge: The Children's Encyclopedia,* Grolier, 1953.

"Nonalogy" is a neologism for "the myth of the magic grandma," from an essay by Jane Marcus on Djuna Barnes's *Nightwood.*

"Picasso to Malraux 1937" is a found poem, from a letter of Picasso's.

"Garment": "When two people have ceased to love, the memory that remains is almost always one of shame." La Rochefoucauld, Maxim 71.

"Superluminal" is a found poem, from an article by James Glanz in *The ScienceTimes,* "Faster Than the Speed of Light, Perhaps, but Not Back to the Future," 30 May 2000, F1.

II. Illusion
"Self-Diagnosis" is a found poem, from the Minnesota Multi-Phasic Inventory.

"Mrs. Johnson": Atropos is the Greek name for one of the three sisters, she who cuts the thread of human life, which Clotho spins and Lachesis measures.

III. Thrift

"Another Minneapolis Poem" responds, in part, to two poems by James Wright, "The Minneapolis Poem" and "A Blessing," and quotes the latter.

"Barbarian" is for Morris Wyszogrod, author of *A Brush With Death,* which includes the well-known Adorno quote.

"Kaddish for Jon" includes quotes (indented, in italics) from *The Song of God: Bhagavad-Gita,* translated by Christopher Isherwood and Swami Prabhavananda; the Kaddish, translated by Leon Weiseltier; and the *Tao Te Ching,* translated by Stephen Mitchell.

"The Thrift Shop of My Dreams": the epigraph is a French saying, source unknown. "Of making many books there is no end," Ecclesiastes 12:12.

Barbara Louise Ungar is an associate professor of English at the College of Saint Rose in Albany, New York. She is the author of a chapbook, *Sequel.* She has published poems in *Salmagundi, The Minnesota Review, The Cream City Review,* and many other journals. She holds degrees from Stanford University, the City College and the Graduate Center of CUNY (City University of New York). She lives in Schuylerville, New York.

Breinigsville, PA USA
14 July 2010
241813BV00002B/25/A